For Pip, Peep, Chip, Drip, Blip, Zip, Zilch, Itsy-Bitsy, Pointy, Freckle, Speckle, Miss Glitter, Particle Pete, Molly Cule, Madame Atom, Dusty, Flurb, Poppy Seed—and Spot, the Dinky Dog

&

Hefty Guy, Mega Mister, Man-o-Saurus, Super-Duper Sue, Colossal Carl, Jupiter, Enormo, and Big Tiny —P. M. & R. C.

Text copyright © 2009 by Patricia Marx
Illustrations copyright © 2009 by Roz Chast

Published by Bloomsbury U.S.A. Children's Books
175 Fifth Avenue, New York, New York 10010

Library of Congress Cataloging-in-Publication Data
Marx, Patricia (Patricia A.)
Dot in Larryland / by Patricia Marx ; illustrated by Roz Chast. — 1st U.S. ed.
p.   cm.
Summary: Teeny, lonely Dot sets out in search of a friend,
while Extra-Large Larry is doing the same.
ISBN-13: 978-1-59990-181-7 · ISBN-10: 1-59990-181-1 (hardcover)
ISBN-13: 978-1-59990-345-3 · ISBN-10: 1-59990-345-8 (reinforced)
[1. Size—Fiction. 2. Loneliness—Fiction. 3. Friendship—Fiction.
4. Humorous stories.] I. Chast, Roz, ill. II. Title.
PZ7.M36823Dot 2009   [E]—dc22   2008030309

Art created with pen and ink and watercolor
Typeset in FelinaSerif
Book design by Daniel Roode

First U.S. Edition 2009
Printed in China
2 4 6 8 10 9 7 5 3 1 (hardcover)
2 4 6 8 10 9 7 5 3 1 (reinforced)

DOT

IN

LARRYLAND

THE BIG (LITTLE) BOOK OF AN

ODD-SIZED FRIENDSHIP

Patricia Marx ✦ illustrated by Roz Chast

BLOOMSBURY
CHILDREN'S
BOOKS

New York ✦ Berlin ✦ London

B et you can't see Dot.

Dot is teenier than a glot. She's smaller than a zot.

And you know what?
Dot is just one jot bigger than invisible,
which is why she is totally miserable.

Dot is lonely. Are you surprised?
It's hard to find friends when you're only Dot-sized.

Then one day last week, when it was pouring,
Dot said to herself,

Dot made her way past the

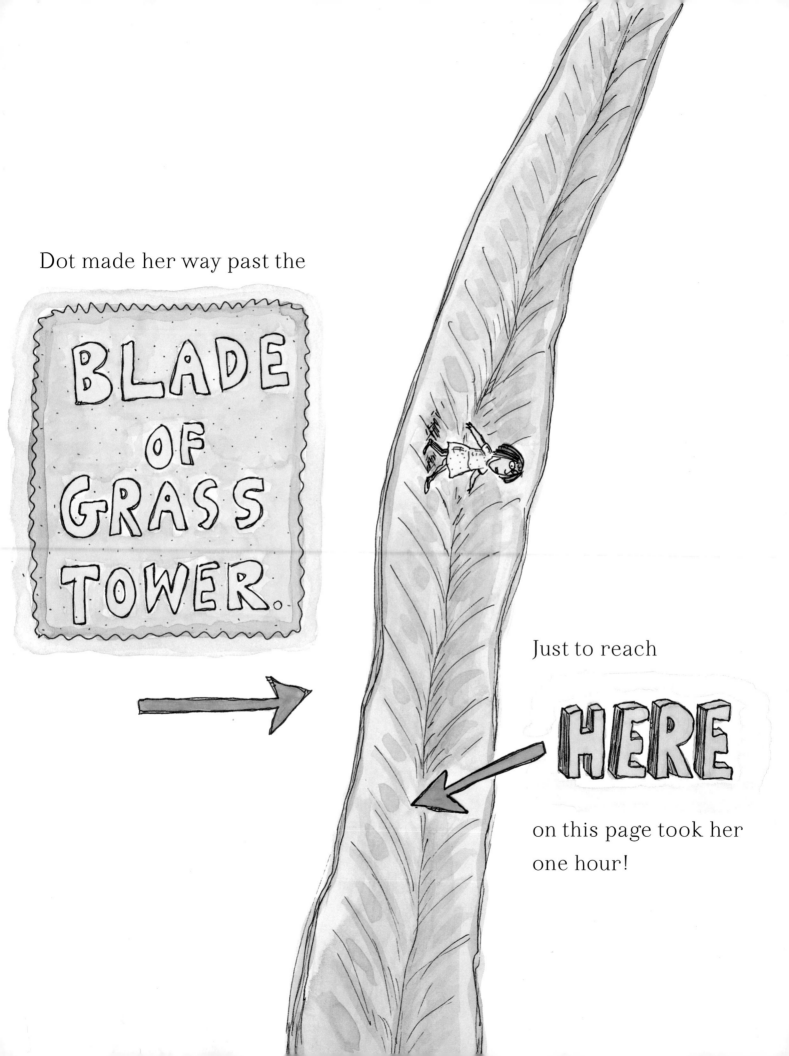

BLADE OF GRASS TOWER.

Just to reach

HERE

on this page took her one hour!

She clambered over this

. . . slid under this

. . . then looked
through this

. . . and what did Dot see?

A land that was covered with itsy-bitsy teensy-weensy milli-micro grains of

Where did Dot go?
Oh, no, no, no, no!
A gust of air . . .

. . . has swept Dot over there.

Dot ended up
in the fur of a pup.
"And who may you be?" asked a flea named Marie.
"I'm Dot," said Dot. "Gee, you're mini like me!
Hey, would some of you fleas like to play ball? I'll pitch."
"We'd love to, Dot, but then who'd make Rex itch?"

Another breeze blew,
and Dot again flew.
(See you later, fleas.)
Where'd the air take her?
Inside a pepper shaker!

STOP!

WE INTERRUPT THIS STORY TO BRING YOU THE

INTERMISSION!

Stretch your legs!

Take a nap! ZZZZZZZZZZZZ

Have a nice, tall glass of water!

Learn lace making!

Fry an egg!

Sing a song, but DON'T BE LONG!

A, B, C, D, E, F, G... Z!

HEY, HOW'D YOU LIKE TO TAKE A LOOK IN ANOTHER PART OF THE BOOK?

Why not? We're here already.

See you later, Dot!

Bet you can't see Larry.

That guy? No, that guy's Harry.

This is Larry. Well, some of Larry.
This is just a little bit of Larry's foot.

Larry is extra large. His toes are so far from his head that if Larry steps in a puddle, he doesn't know it till tomorrow.

Extra-Large Larry is lonesome. In a really **BIG** way.

Then one day, Extra-Large Larry said to himself,

Which is why Larry said to the house at 66 Edgars Lane,

"Impossible," said the house. "I'm stuck here, in charge of the Johnsons' stuff."

"What about you?" Larry asked the weeping willow. "Let's play hide-and-seek!"
But the tree was too busy weeping to do anything but cry.

Finally, Larry stood on his extra-large tippy toes and said to a cloud passing by, "Hey, want to hear a great joke?"
"Not now," said the cloud. "I'm late for a burst. Toodle-oo."

Will Larry *ever* find a friend?

Bet you're thinking: Aha! This is the part where Dot and Larry become best buddies and live happily ever after.

Better bet again. Junk like that only happens in books.

HERE'S THE ABSOLUTELY TRUE, NO-FOOLING-AROUND WAY THEY MET:

One morning, at the diner, Extra-Large Larry was having his usual breakfast.

Except today, when Larry spiced up that sixteenth burger, something unusual came sneezing out of the pepper shaker.

Could this be the end of Dot?

Dot

"Whoa!" said Dot. "As you can see—I'm no big deal.
Still it isn't my dream to be part of your meal.
So, please, big guy, I hate to kvetch, but—
could you try not to drown me in all of that ketchup?
And one last thing. I don't mean to be rude.
My name is Dot. You're a nice-looking dude."

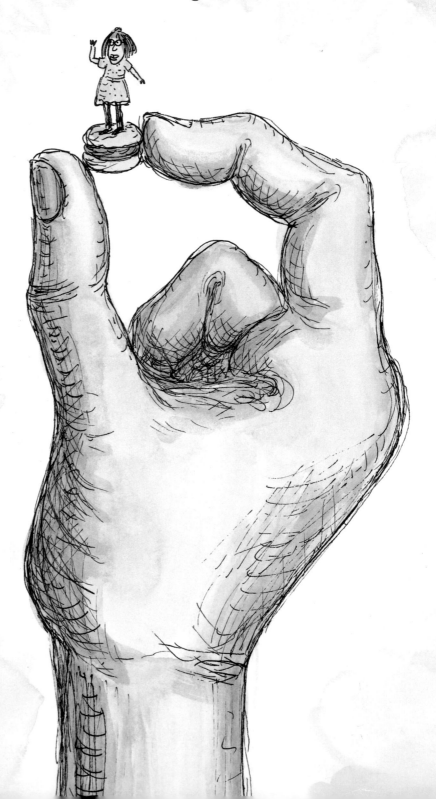

"I'm Larry," said Larry. "I'm large and I'm lonely."

"I'm teeny," said Dot. "I'm a one and an only."

"Same here," said Larry. "Would you like something to eat?"

"As long as it's not me," said Dot, "it'd be a treat."

And so, to make a long story short and vice versa,
Things got lots better, instead of lots worsa.

A sky-high guy
meets a glot-like dot,
and they become right-sized friends
till the end of . . .